Apollo Has a Bad Day

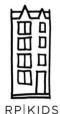

RP|KIDS
PHILADELPHIA · LONDON

Books published by Running Press are available at special discounts for bulk purchases
in the United States by corporations, institutions, and other organizations. For more information, please contact
the Special Markets Department at the Perseus Books Group, 2300 Chestnut Street, Suite 200, Philadelphia, PA 19103,
or call (800) 810-4145, ext. 5000, or e-mail special.markets@perseusbooks.com.

ISBN 978-0-7624-5022-0

Library of Congress Control Number: 2013939233

9 8 7 6 5 4 3 2 1
Digit on the right indicates the number of this printing

Art adapted by Paige Pooler
Designed by Frances J Soo Ping Chow
Text adapted by Ellie O'Ryan
Edited by Marlo Scrimizzi
Typography: Vag Rounded and Univers

Published by Running Press Kids
An Imprint of Running Press Book Publishers
A Member of the Perseus Books Group
2300 Chestnut Street
Philadelphia, PA 19103–4371

Visit us on the web!
www.runningpress.com/kids

Outside, the first stars were starting to appear. But there was still a little time to play before bed. Apollo knew exactly what he wanted to do: finish building his block tower.

"There we go!" Apollo said as he carefully added a block to the tippy-top of the tower.

"Apollo! Apollo! Apollo!" Squacky yelled. "I have a 'mergency. My ball went under the bed again, and I can't get it out. I need you!"

Apollo sighed. "I kind of wanna finish my tower," he replied.

"Did you hear me when I said 'mergency?" Squacky said. "'Mergency means no-I-cannot-wait-at-all!"

"Okay, okay. Let's go," Apollo said.

Apollo followed Squacky over to Cowbella's bed.
"It's under there," Squacky told him. "In the farthest, darkest,
impossiblest corner!"

Apollo got down on his stomach and wiggled under the bed. "Got it!" he announced. Then Apollo threw the ball across the room. Squacky laughed as he chased it.

"I'm coming out," Apollo told the other Pajanimals.

THUNK!

"Ouch!" Apollo groaned. "I hit my head on the bed. It really, really hurts!"

The Pajanimals hurried over to him.
"Oh no, Apollo!" Cowbella cried. "I think you need a wet towel on your head."
Squacky's eyes lit up. "Don't move!" he exclaimed as he dashed off.

When Squacky returned, he was wearing his blankie like a cape. "Da-da-da-daaaa," he sang. "Super Squacky is on it!"

Then Squacky rushed off to the bathroom. "Stand back," he yelled as he threw something at Apollo. "Here it comes!"

SPLAT!

A cold, wet towel landed right on Apollo's head! It didn't feel very nice.

"Is that better?" Squacky asked hopefully.

Apollo didn't answer right away. Finally, he said, "No. I think I just want to finish building my block tower . . . by myself."

Apollo was still working on his tower when Dad called out, "Five more minutes till bedtime, Pajanimals. And sorry about your sheets, Apollo."

"My sheets?" Apollo asked. He hurried over to his bed, which was covered with plain white sheets.

"Remember?" Sweet Pea Sue said. "Your rocket-ship sheets are being washed."

"What?" shrieked Squacky. "But you always sleep with your rocket-ship sheets! This is a disaster! 'Mergency! 'Mergency! 'Mergency!"

Apollo didn't say anything as he sadly went back to his blocks.

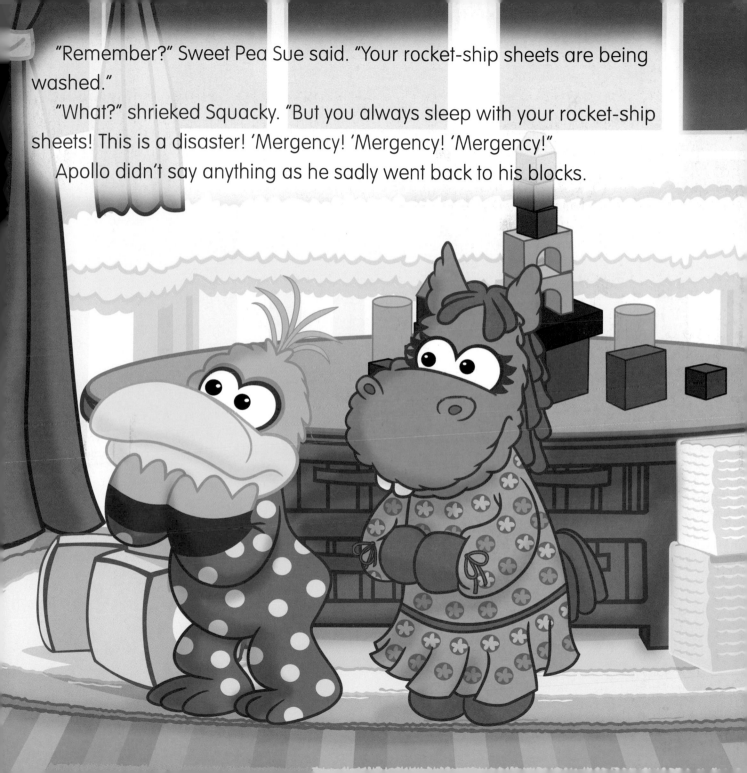

At last, Apollo's block tower was done. He was so proud of it. "Phew!" he exclaimed. "It's finally finished!"

Suddenly, Cowbella twirled past him. "Whoa! Careful of my block tower." Apollo warned her.

Then Sweet Pea Sue bustled by. "Watch my tower!" Apollo said.

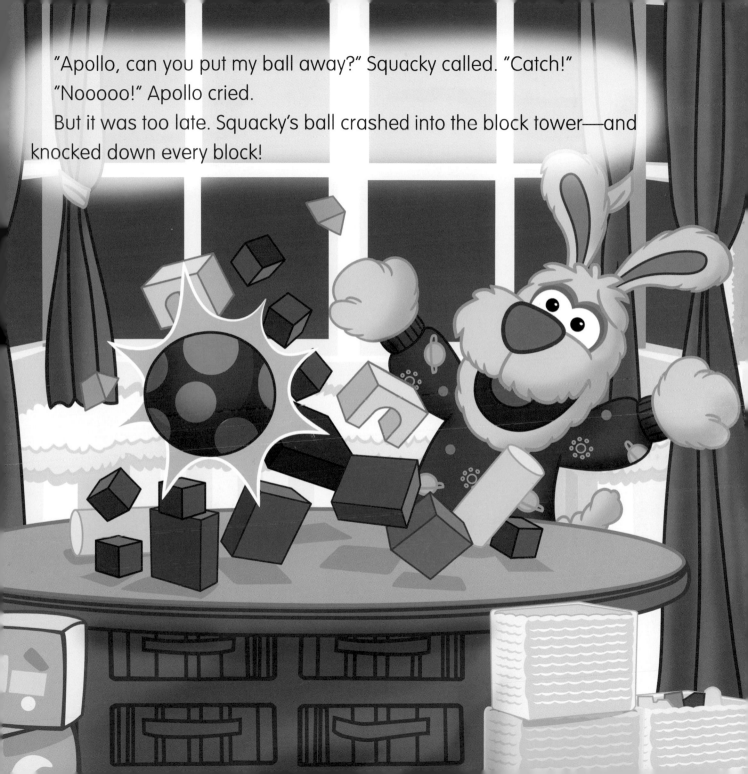

"Apollo, can you put my ball away?" Squacky called. "Catch!"

"Nooooo!" Apollo cried.

But it was too late. Squacky's ball crashed into the block tower—and knocked down every block!

Apollo was so upset that he started shaking. He stomped into the bathroom and slammed the door.

"I'm really sorry, Apollo," Squacky said through the bathroom door.

But Apollo didn't answer.

"Are you okay, Apollo?" asked Sweet Pea Sue.

Finally, Apollo opened the door. "No, okay is what I am not!" he exclaimed. "My head feels bumpy. My stomach is squnchy. . . . I think I am MAD . . . and also sad."

Soon it was time for bed.

"Good night, Pajanimals. Sleep tight. See you in the morning light," said Mom.

"Good night, Mom," the Pajanimals said.

In his cozy bed, Apollo tossed and turned. Then he sighed and sat up. "I can't sleep. I still feel mad and sad. I had a bad day! I think I need some help."

Squacky, Cowbella, and Sweet Pea Sue climbed onto Apollo's bed. Then his bed rose into the air!

"Ready?" Apollo asked.

"Ready!" said the Pajanimals.

"Let's bundle up, snuggle up, huggle up, and go!"

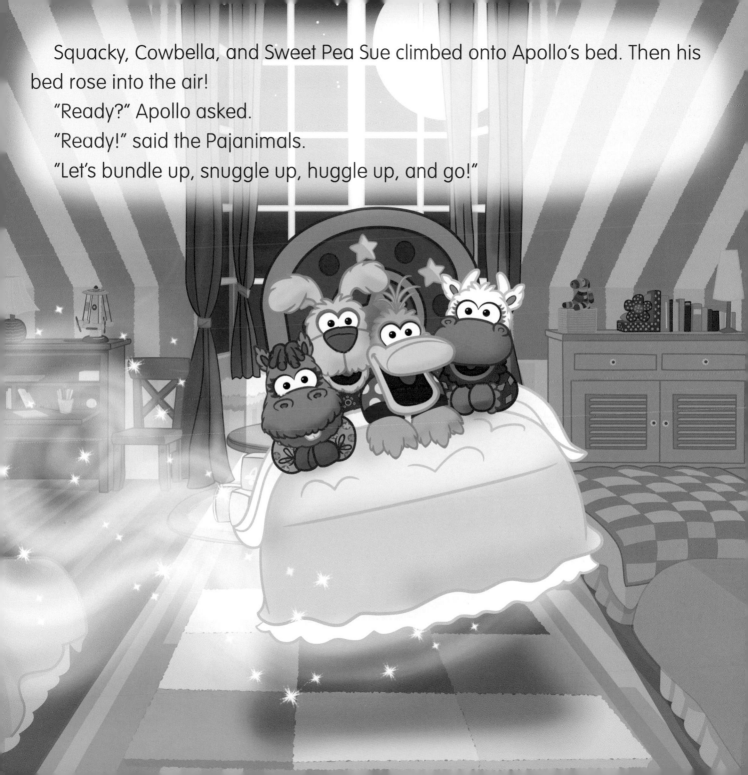

Then Apollo's bed turned into a rocket ship. It flew all the way to the Moon!

"Welcome, Pajanimals," the Moon said. "What brings you to my night sky tonight?"

"Let me tell you," Squacky said. "Apollo bumped his head on the bed, and then his sheets were in the laundry, and his block tower got knocked down."

"Well, Apollo, it sounds like you had a bad day," the Moon said.

"I did," Apollo replied sadly. "And I can't sleep because I keep thinking about it."

"I understand," the Moon told Apollo. "One of the magical things about sleeping is that it washes away the day. When you wake up, it's tomorrow, and tomorrow you will feel better."

"I will?" asked Apollo.

"Yes, because tomorrow is a brand new day," the Moon promised.

Apollo smiled. "I like that idea," he said. "I can't wait for tomorrow!"

"Oh good!" the Moon chuckled. "Now it's time to go home, Pajanimals. Good night."

"Good night, Moon. Thanks! See you soon!" the Pajanimals replied.

The Pajanimals went to bed as soon as they got home. But Squacky had something important to tell Apollo. "I'm really, really sorry about your block tower, Apollo," he whispered.

"Tomorrow, do you want to build a new block tower together?" Apollo whispered back.

"Oh yes!" Squacky said happily.

Then all the Pajanimals fell asleep. They couldn't wait for a brand new day!